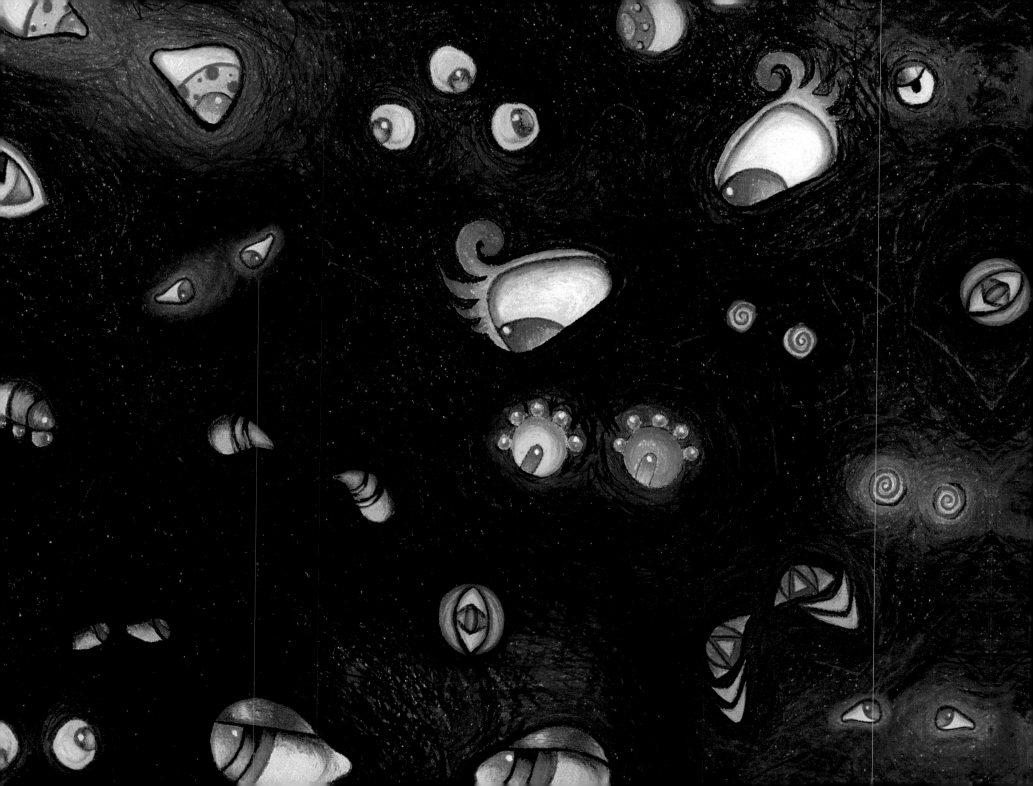

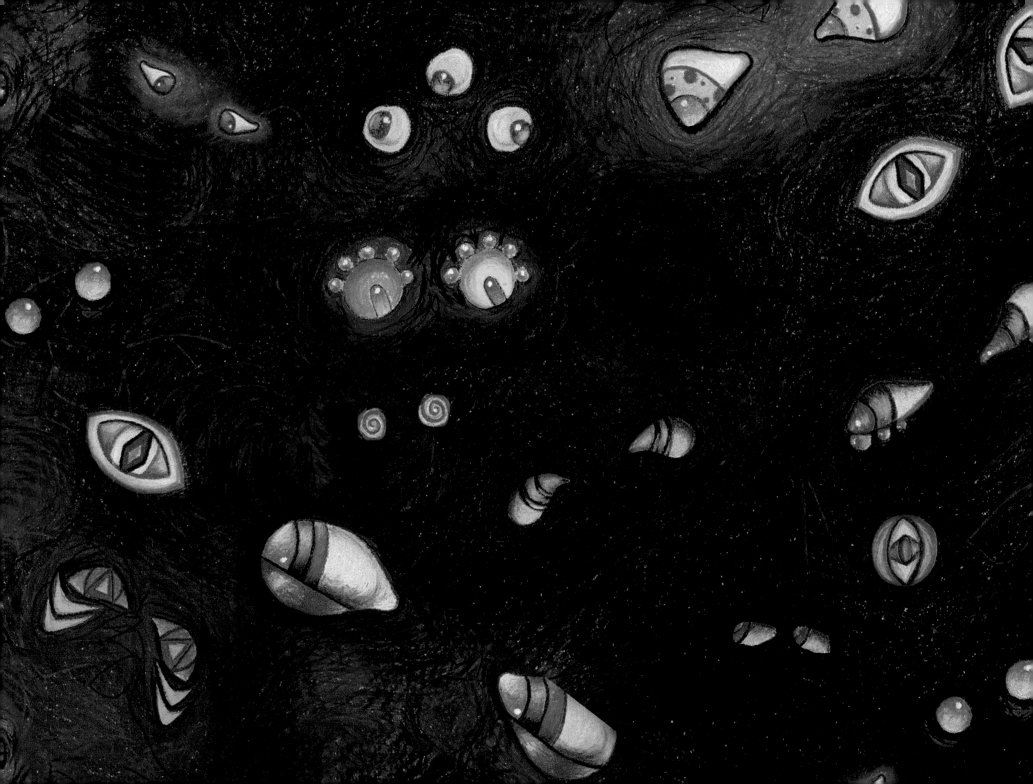

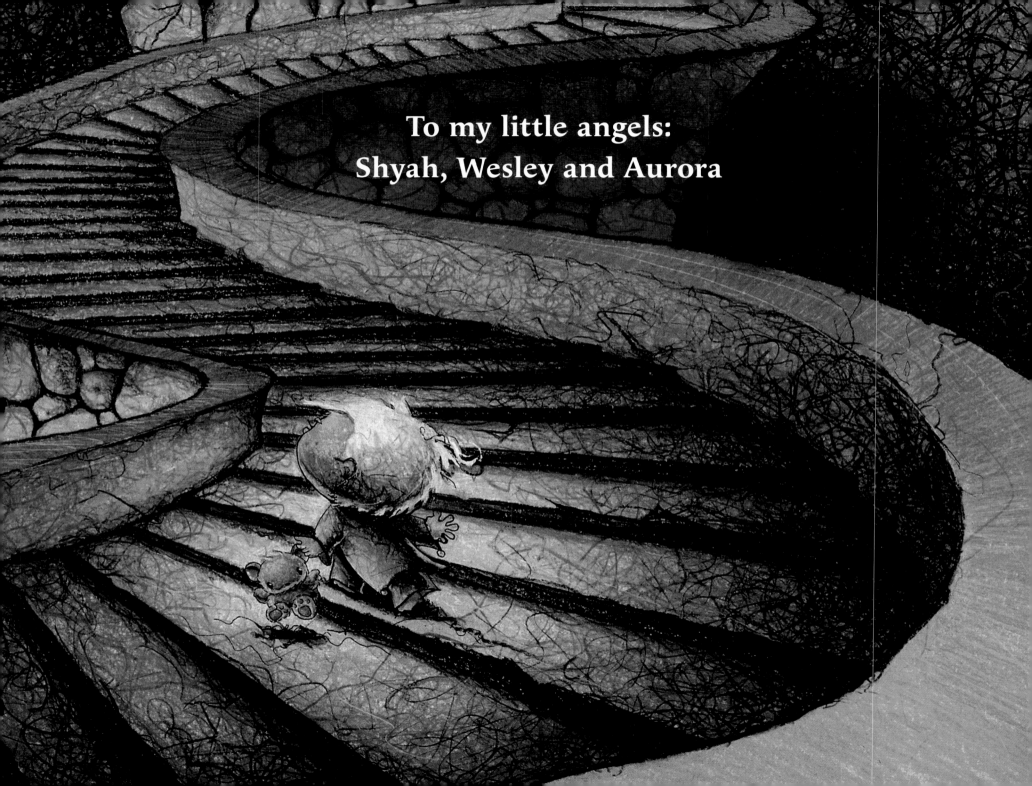

To my little angels:
Shyah, Wesley and Aurora

This book is given with love

Prince Applehead
HUMPLEDINK

Written and Illustrated
by Pearl Preis

One stormy night, in a old, drafty castle,

by a big, crackling fire...

there sat a little prince

named Apple Head Humpledink.

Prince Apple Head Humpledink

was much too scared

to sleep in his room,

and it was well past his bedtime.

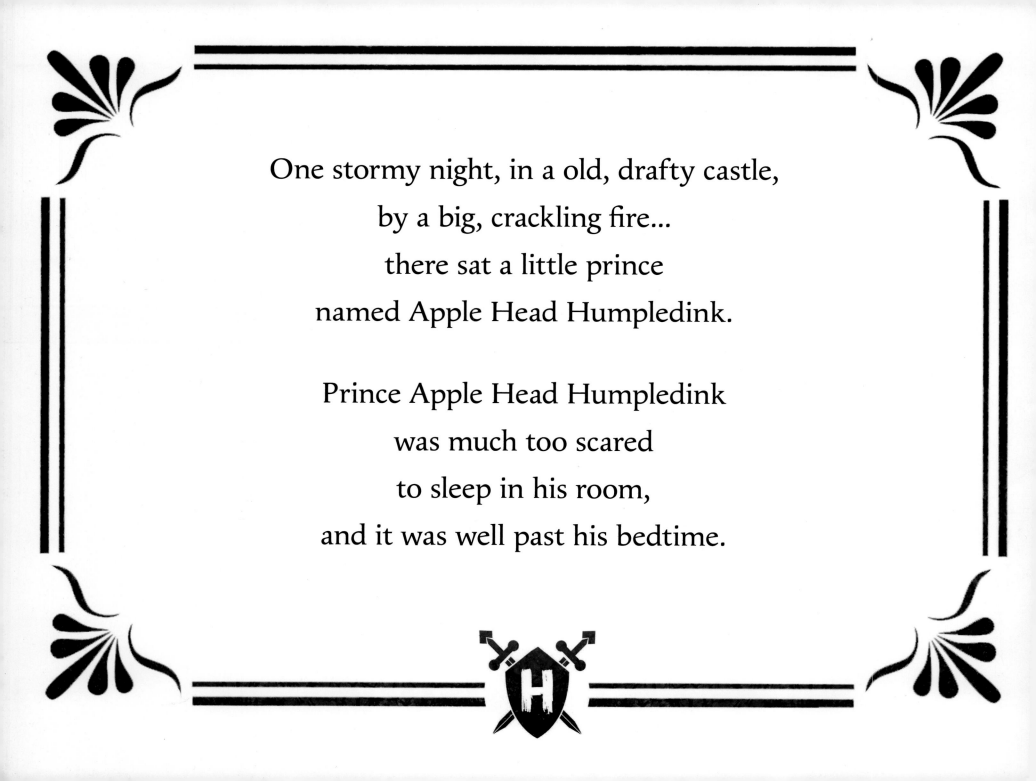

"Just a few minutes more?" he would ask.

"You've been asking that for hours," replied the King,
"it's time to go to bed, little prince."

Prince Apple Head Humpledink spoke in a whisper,
"but I can't go to bed...there are **THINGS** in my room."

"For the one hundredth time," said the King,
"there are no **THINGS** in your room."

"Oh yes there are!" the prince cried, then he ran to the Queen,
hoping that she would agree with him.

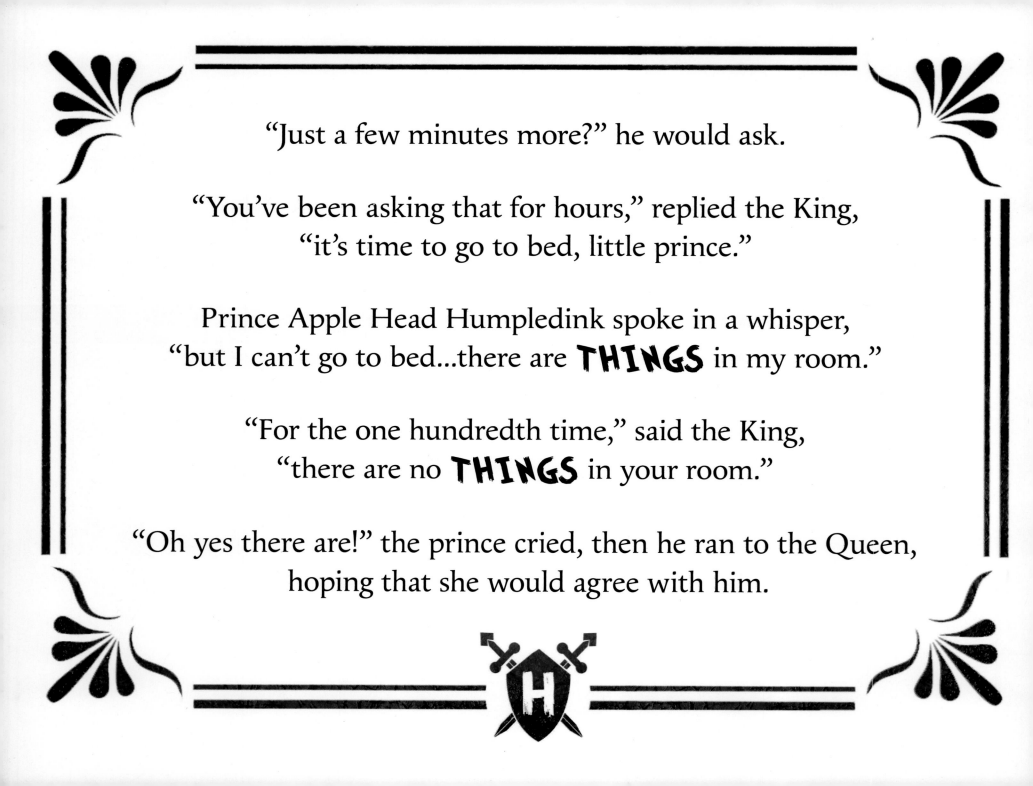

"Let me tell you a secret," began the Queen,
"once you show those **THINGS** that you are not afraid,
those **THINGS** will go away forever. Just give it a try."

"Okay," the prince sniffled, then climbed the
long, lonely staircase up to his room,
"but this could be the last time you'll ever see me!"

"Good night and good luck!" called the King and Queen.

At the top of the stairs,

Prince Apple Head Humpledink

tiptoed to his tall, narrow door and opened it slowly...

He listened very carefully...

but he didn't hear a thing.

Then he peeked inside cautiously...

but he didn't see a thing.

KA-RASH!!!

A big flash of lightning filled the room,
and Prince Apple Head Humpledink jumped into his bed,
hiding under the the safety of his covers.

And that's when he heard it...
a knock on his balcony door!

He grabbed his trusty flashlight,
that he hid under his pillow, and turned it on
so he could see the **THINGS** that were there...

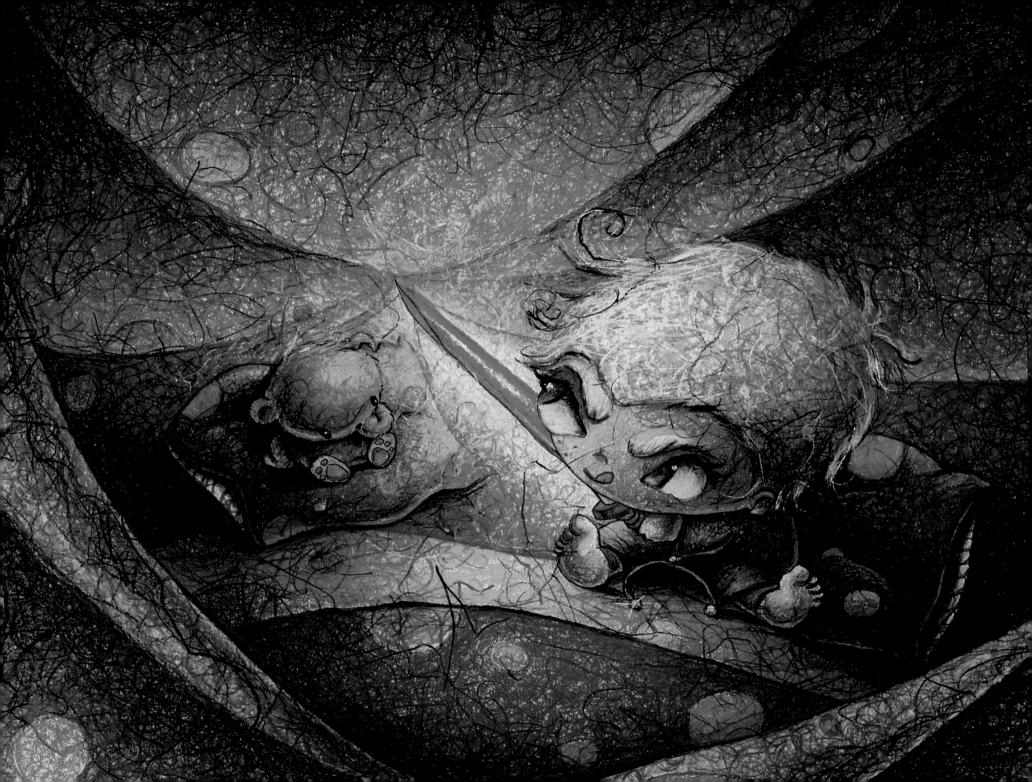

KA-RASH!!!

More lightning filled the room,
and Prince Apple Head Humpledink screamed
as he jumped bravely out of bed...
and threw open the balcony door
to confront the **THINGS.**

"I'm not afraid of you anymore!
So stop that knocking on my door!"

SLASH! SLASH! SLASH!

He swung his light beam at all the little **THINGS**
that lived outside his balcony door,
making leaves, branches, and flowers
go flying through the air.

When it was all over,
Prince Apple Head Humpledink
stood on top of these **THINGS** and smiled.

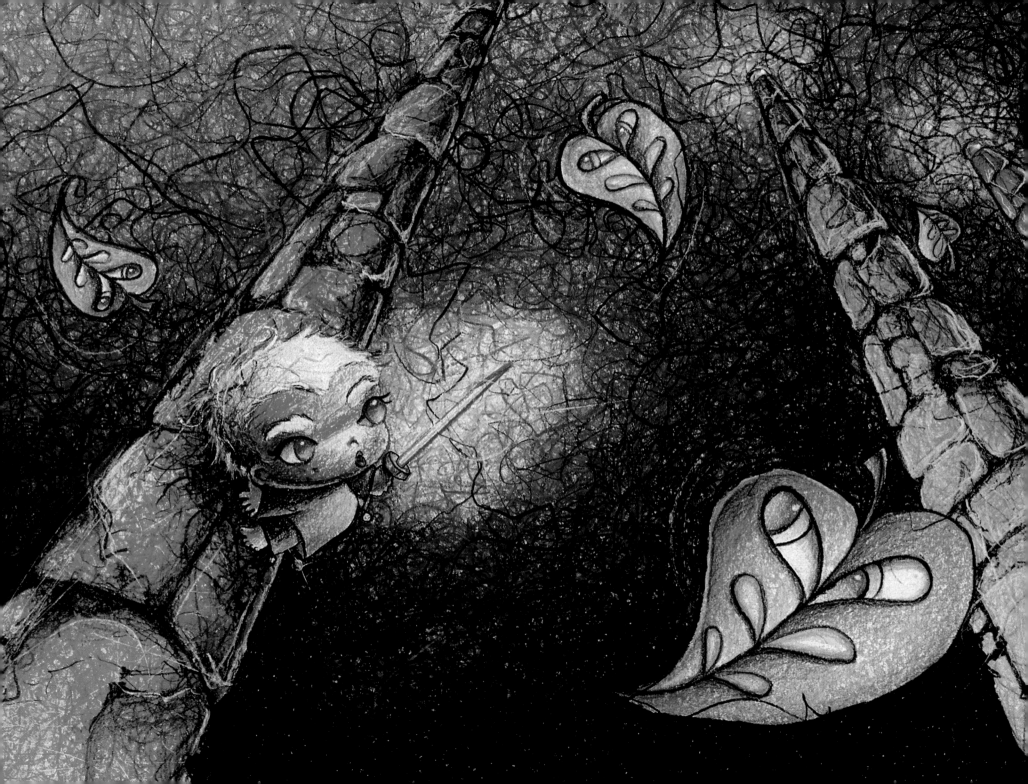

KA-RASH!!!

The lightning came again!
This time, it showed the eyes of all the **THINGS**
that lived under Prince Apple Head Humpledink's bed.

"Aha!" yelled the Prince as he dove down after them,
"I'm not afraid of you any more!
So stop that scratching on my floor!"

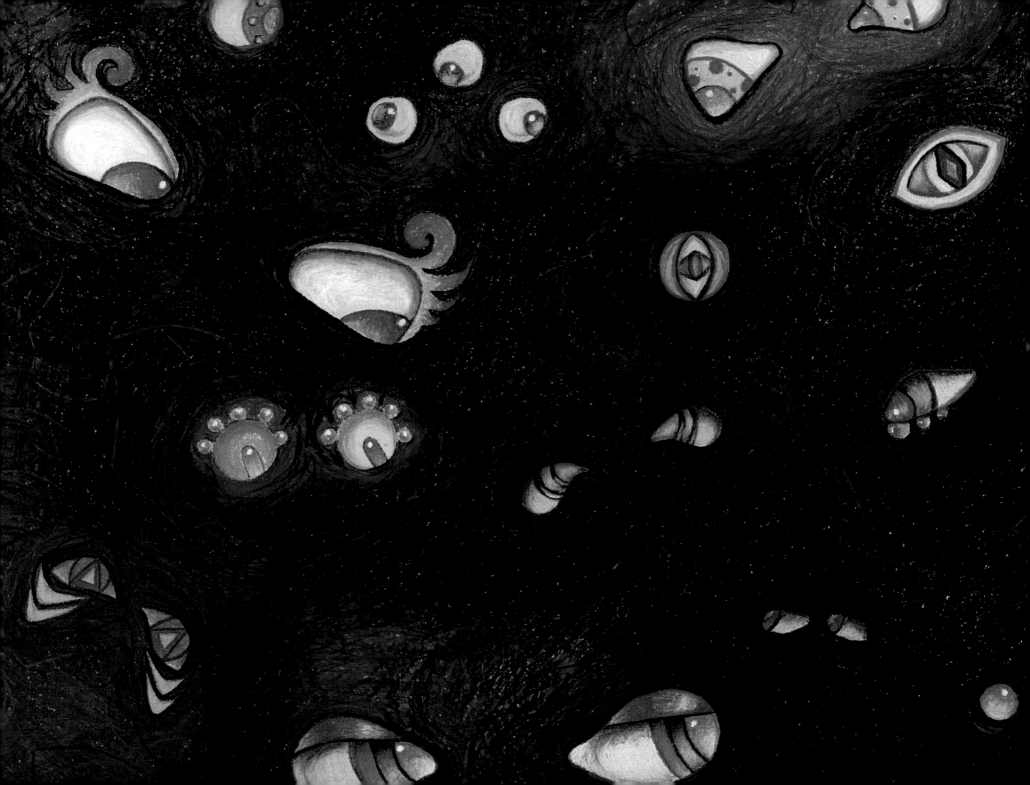

SWISH! SWISH! SWISH!

He swung his light sword at all the **THINGS**
that lived under his bed,
making marbles, crayons, and shoes
go flying all over.

When it was all over,

Prince Apple Head Humpledink

lay there on his bedroom floor,

exhausted from fighting all of these **THINGS.**

BRRRA-BOOOOOOM!!!

The thunder crashed loudly and angrily...

And Prince Apple Head Humpledink sat up

as he heard his closet door rattle.

He grabbed hold of his trusty sword,
and yelled at the **THINGS**
that lived inside of his closet...

"I'm not afraid of you anymore!
So stop that rattling at my door!"

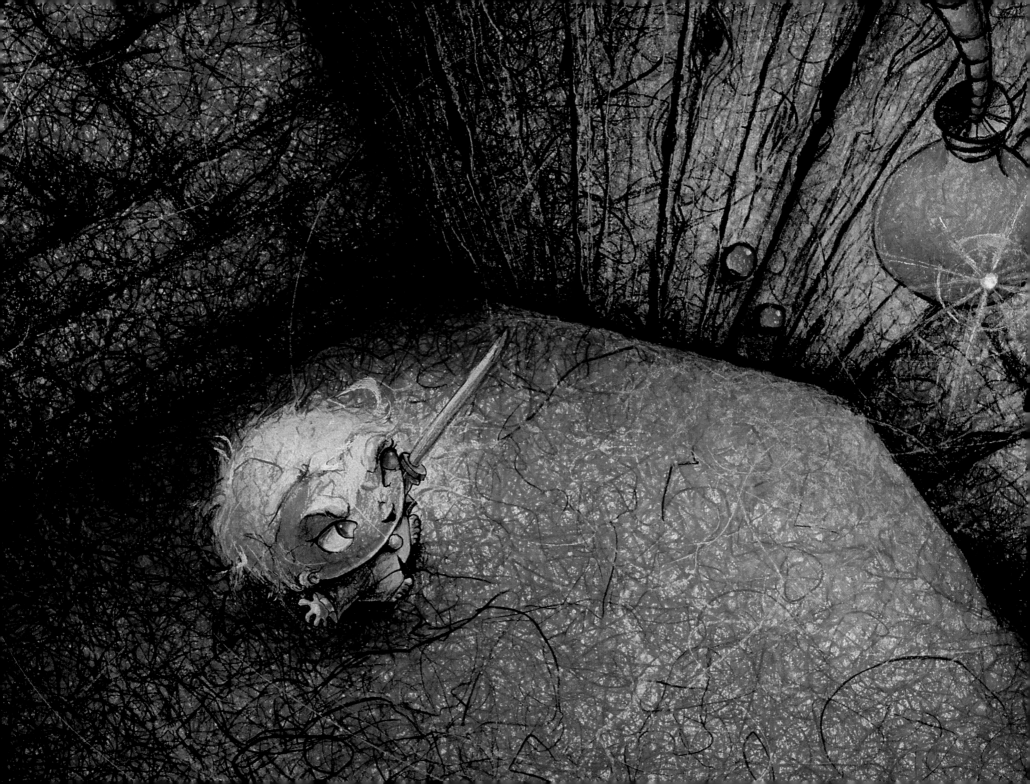

SWOOSH! SWOOSH! SWOOSH!

He swung his light beam at all the **THINGS**
that lived just behind his closet door,
making coats, shirts, and hangers
go flying along the floor.

The colorful, terrible closet **THING** and the Prince
fought long and hard in the room,
as the lightning flashed and the thunder boomed.

When it was all over,

Prince Apple Head Humpledink

collapsed on top of the closet **THING**,

and that's when realized

that of all the **THINGS** he was afraid of...

Were just the **THINGS**

in his room all along!

When the King and Queen
finally went up the long, lonely staircase
to the tall, narrow door
of Prince Apple Head Humpledink's bedroom,
and poked their heads in to say good night,
they heard him whisper these words...

I'm not afraid of you anymore.

All you **THINGS** behind my door.

I can now go to bed and fall asleep soon,

Because there are no more **THINGS** inside my room.

THE END

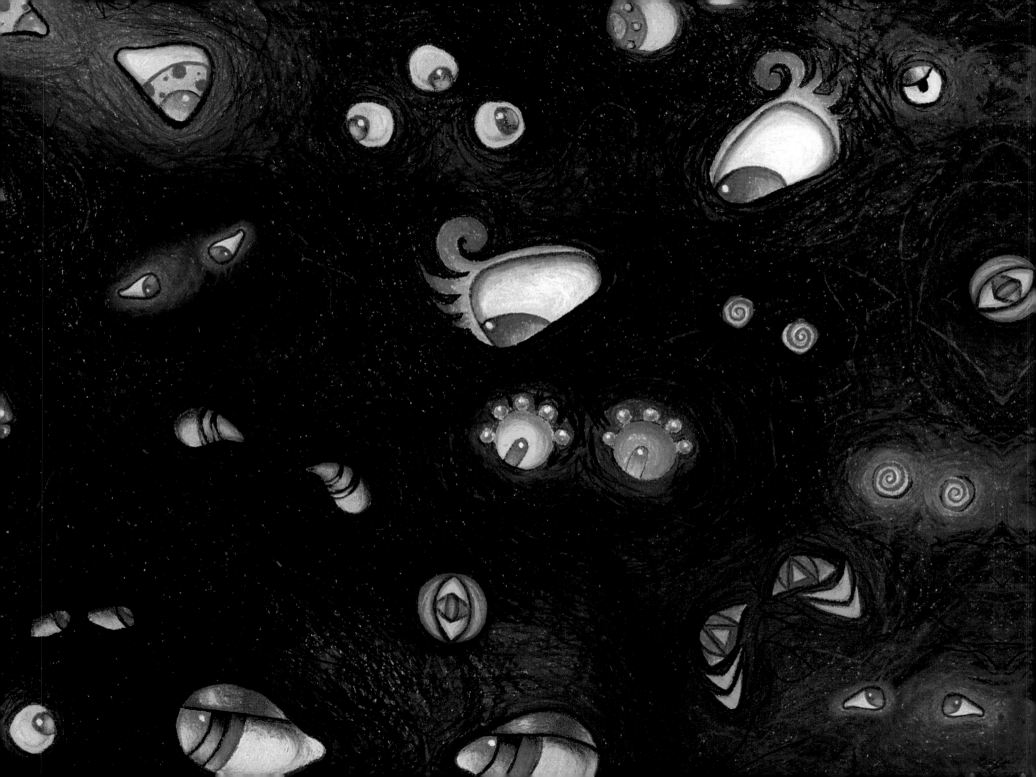